2008

W9-BTR-897

WITHDRAWN

The
Tiara
Club

Also in the Tiara Club

Princess Charlotte *and the* Birthday Ball

Princess Katie *and the* Silver Pony

Princess Daisy *and the* Dazzling Dragon

Princess Alice *and the* Magical Mirror

Princess Emily *and the* Substitute Fairy

VIVIAN FRENCH

The Tiara Club

Princess Sophia
AND THE
Sparkling Surprise

ILLUSTRATED BY SARAH GIBB

KATHERINE TEGEN BOOKS
An Imprint of HarperCollins*Publishers*

The Tiara Club: Princess Sophia and the Sparkling Surprise

Text copyright © 2007 by Vivian French

Illustrations copyright © 2007 by Sarah Gibb

www.harpercollinschildrens.com

Library of Congress Cataloging-in-Publication Data

French, Vivian.

Princess Sophia and the sparkling surprise / by Vivian French ;
illustrated by Sarah Gibb.

p. cm. — (The Tiara Club ; 5)

Summary: As Princess Sophia and her friends design and create
their own ball gowns for the Princess Academy Surprise, a group of
snobs led by Princess Perfecta plots to ruin them.

ISBN-10: 0-06-112438-9 (trade bdg.)

ISBN-13: 978-0-06-112438-9 (trade bdg.)

ISBN-10: 0-06-112437-0 (pbk. bdg.)

ISBN-13: 978-0-06-112437-2 (pbk. bdg.)

[1. Princesses—Fiction. 2. Behavior—Fiction. 3. Dressmaking—
Fiction. 4. Schools—Fiction.] I. Gibb, Sarah, ill. II. Title.

PZ7.F88917Pris 2007   2006020330

[Fic]—dc22   CIP

                                                                        AC

Typography by Amy Ryan

1 2 3 4 5 6 7 8 9 10

❖

First U.S. edition, 2007

For Princess Jenny and
her lovely mum too, xxx
—V.F.

For mum and dad,
with love
—S.G.

The Royal Palace Academy
for the Preparation of Perfect Princesses
(Known to our students as "The Princess Academy")

OUR SCHOOL MOTTO:
*A Perfect Princess always thinks of others before herself,
and is kind, caring, and truthful.*

We offer the complete curriculum for all princesses, including:

How to Talk to a Dragon

Creative Cooking for Perfect Palace Parties

Wishes, and How to Use Them Wisely

Designing and Creating the Perfect Ball Gown

Avoiding Magical Mistakes

Descending a Staircase as if Floating on Air

Our principal, Queen Gloriana, is present at all times, and students are in the excellent care of the school Fairy Godmother.

VISITING TUTORS AND EXPERTS INCLUDE:

KING PERCIVAL *(Dragons)*

LADY VICTORIA *(Banquets)*

QUEEN MOTHER MATILDA *(Etiquette, Posture, and Poise)*

THE GRAND HIGH DUCHESS DELIA *(Fashion)*

We award tiara points to encourage
our princesses toward the next level.
Each princess who earns enough points
in her first year is welcomed to the
Tiara Club and presented with a silver tiara.

Tiara Club princesses are invited to return
next year to Silver Towers, our very special
residence for Perfect Princesses, where they
may continue their education at a higher level.

PLEASE NOTE:
Princesses are expected to arrive
at the Academy with a *minimum* of:

TWENTY BALL GOWNS
*(with all necessary hoops,
petticoats, etc.)*

TWELVE DAY-DRESSES

SEVEN GOWNS
*suitable for garden parties
and other special daytime
occasions*

TWELVE TIARAS

DANCING SHOES
five pairs

VELVET SLIPPERS
three pairs

RIDING BOOTS
two pairs

*Cloaks, muffs, stoles, gloves,
and other essential
accessories, as required*

Hello! My name is Princess Sophia, and I'm so pleased you're keeping us company here at the Princess Academy.

Have you met the others from Rose Room? There's Alice, and Katie, and Daisy, and Charlotte, and Emily, and we've been best friends ever since we met on the very first day of school. We take care of each other—a very good thing when there are princesses like Perfecta around.

She's so mean! Some day she'll learn that being a real princess is all about being kind and truthful and thinking about others before you think of yourself. But until then, Princess Perfecta means trouble!

Chapter One

We were just finishing breakfast, and Charlotte was saying how boring it was because there were no fancy balls or parties to look forward to, when suddenly Fairy G. appeared out of nowhere in a cloud of silver sparkles. (Fairy G. is the school's fairy godmother.)

Fairy G. dusted away the sparkles and beamed at us.

"I've got a very special treat for you first-year princesses," she said.

"Queen Gloriana has canceled your usual lessons, and you're to spend all day in the Sewing Room with the Grand High Duchess Delia!" She looked as if she was expecting a huge cheer . . . but there wasn't one.

Nobody said anything, until Perfecta raised her hand. "Excuse me, Fairy G.," she said, "but you aren't expecting us to do any *sewing*, are you?" She made it sound like the worst thing you could ever ever do—worse than eating worms!

Fairy G. gave Perfecta a chilly look. "Of *course* I am, Perfecta," she said. "The Grand High Duchess is the best needlewoman in the whole kingdom! Her designs for ballgowns and dresses are truly wonderful, and you're very, *very* lucky she's agreed to spend a day here."

Perfecta made a disgusted face. "My mother and father would be furious if they thought I was making my own dresses." She sneered. "That's for servants to do!"

I held my breath and waited for Fairy G. to explode, but she didn't. Well . . . not quite.

"I would like to remind you, Princess Perfecta," Fairy G. said,

and she sounded very stern, "that tiara points are won *and* lost in many different ways. Be very careful!"

She turned to the rest of us. "Hurry up, now. Duchess Delia is waiting for you. Make sure you wash your hands before you make your way to the sewing room. I'm sure we'll all have a lovely day!"

And she disappeared, but this time in the usual way—through the dining room door.

As soon as she was gone, we all started talking at once.

"I'm hopeless at sewing," Princess Katie wailed. "I tried to make a dress for one of my dolls once, and it was awful!"

"Me too," Princess Charlotte said. "I always sew the wrong pieces to each other."

"So do I!" said Princess Emily.

"And I always prick my fingers," Princess Daisy said.

"It might be okay," Princess Alice said cheerfully. "My grandmama makes quite a lot of my clothes, and I help her sometimes. It's fun—we think of all kinds of ways we can use old velvet curtains or leftover pieces of satin from Grandpapa's royal sashes."

"*Old velvet curtains?*" Perfecta and her nasty friend Princess Floreen were standing right beside

Alice, and staring at her in the most despising way.

Alice giggled. "Yes! One of my most favorite winter ballgowns was made of heavenly red velvet from the throne room!"

Perfecta put her arm around Floreen's shoulder. "If you ask me, Floreen," she said with a sniff,

"princesses who are so poor that they have to make their dresses from curtains shouldn't be allowed to come to the Academy! I mean, we might just as well invite in beggars and tramps!

"Real princesses are rich, *and* they have servants. How on earth can you join the Tiara Club if you

haven't even got a sewing maid?" Perfecta tossed her head, and was just about to march away when I grabbed Alice and swept her past Perfecta and out into the middle of the dining hall.

Chapter Two

I do know it is *not* being a Perfect Princess to go around grabbing people. I really do! But Perfecta made me so mad I couldn't help it. For a second, I didn't care one bit about tiara points—or even the Tiara Club. I held Alice's hand,

and I said in my *very* loudest voice, "Sometimes Princess Perfecta is so stupid! The richest princess in the whole wide world would *never* be as special as *you* are, Alice! Being a Perfect Princess has nothing to do with money—it's all about being

kind, and truthful, and taking care of other people, and thinking about other people before yourself. But I don't think princesses like Perfecta and Floreen will ever be smart enough to understand such things!" And then I whirled Alice out of the dining hall and into the corridor outside.

"Wow!" Alice said. "That told her! And right in front of everybody too!"

I leaned against the wall and tried to look calm and graceful, the way a Perfect Princess should, but my heart was beating really fast. "She deserved it," I said. "How could she say that? She's such a snob!"

Alice gave me a hug. "Thank you *so* much for standing up for me! But do you know what? I don't care what she says—I don't think she's worth our time." Alice peered back into the dining hall. "Here

come the rest of the Rose Room Princesses!"

Alice was right. Charlotte and the others came hurrying out of the dining hall to join us.

"What's Perfecta doing?" Alice wanted to know.

"She's absolutely furious,"

Charlotte said. "She and Floreen are whispering together—they're probably planning some horrible revenge!"

I'd calmed down a bit, but part of me was beginning to worry. It wasn't perfect *or* princessy to call someone stupid in front of everyone in the first year. But, I told myself, Perfecta *had* been so mean to Alice.

We went off to the bathroom to wash our hands. As we were coming out, I saw Perfecta and Floreen walking toward me.

All at once, a sort of fight broke out inside my head. Have you ever had that happen? Part of me wanted to walk right past Perfecta and pretend she wasn't there, but another part of me was saying I should smile at her as if nothing had happened, and *another* part was wondering if I should apologize.

I didn't have to decide. Perfecta

came straight up to me.

"Do you know what you are, Princess Sophia?" she hissed. "You're a horrible goody-goody! You're so sugary-sweet and nice as pie you make me *sick*! But don't think you can get away with it! Just because

you think you're so perfect, that doesn't mean you can pick on me in front of everybody! You're a horrible la-di-da show-off!" And then she stormed into the bathroom, slamming the door so loudly that bits of plaster fell off the ceiling. Floreen scuttled after her, and as she vanished she squeaked, "And don't worry—we're going to get you back!"

"Oh, dear," I said.

"Just ignore her," Alice said. "Come on! Let's go and see what this Grand High Duchess has lined up for us."

"She'd never dare do anything

anyway," Daisy said. "Whatever would Queen Gloriana and Fairy G. say if they found one princess sticking pins into another?"

That made me laugh. We bounced into the Sewing Room to find Duchess Delia and Fairy G. arranging huge piles of gorgeous fabrics on the tables . . . and when I say "gorgeous," I really, *really* mean it. I'd never seen anything like it in my whole life. There were smooth, plushy velvets; and the softest, fluffiest wools; and rolls and rolls of crunchy petticoat lace . . . and they were all as white as the cleanest, crispest snow! It looked utterly magical.

"Do come in, my dears," Duchess Delia said, as she pointed to an empty table. Most of the rest of our year were already sitting at the other tables whispering to each

other, and I just knew they were talking about my fight with Perfecta. Then the Sewing Room door opened again, and the whispering stopped dead, so I knew Perfecta had come in. Do you know what? I felt so uncomfortable I almost burst into tears.

Chapter Three

I think Fairy G. must have known that something was going on, because she always does . . . but she deals with things in her own way. Even so, I was shocked when she made Perfecta and Floreen sit with us at our table. I waited for Perfecta to say something, and she did, but it was not at all what I'd expected. She made sure Duchess Delia was looking, and then she said in a sweet little voice, "Oh, Alice! How lovely! You know all about sewing, don't you? I'm honored to sit next to you!"

Alice didn't know *what* to do! She sort of gasped. "Um . . . er . . . thank you."

Fairy G. gave Perfecta such an odd look. Then she beamed at the rest of us. "Now, let's give our special guest an enormous Princess Academy welcome!"

We all clapped, and I was really wondering what Perfecta was up to.

Duchess Delia peered at us over her spectacles, and Fairy G. coughed. "Ahem. Perhaps you'd like to tell the princesses about their task for today, Duchess?"

The Duchess nodded. "Oh, I would! Now, girls, you're each going to design and make your very own winter ballgown, and you'll wear it to the Princess Academy Surprise—"

"Harrrrrumph!!!"

She was interrupted by a huge roar from Fairy G., but it was too late. We were all sitting bolt upright, our eyes shining. A *surprise*?

Katie raised her hand. "Please—dear, *dear* Fairy G.—What surprise?"

Fairy G. folded her arms. "You'll just have to wait and see!" she said

firmly. "It won't be a surprise if we tell you!"

Duchess Delia giggled. "Oh, dear me," she said, "I'm so sorry! But now, girls—here are a few of my winter designs to give you some ideas. I've asked some of the Tiara Club Princesses to model for me." She clapped her hands, and we gasped.

A line of beautiful princesses came sweeping in through the Sewing Room door, wearing the most glorious dresses you've ever seen. Our eyes opened as wide as saucers! Normally we never see any of the Tiara Club Princesses, because they stay in the Silver Towers on the other side of the valley, and they don't have anything to do with us.

Alice's big sister is there, and Alice sees her only during the holidays. One by one, each princess sailed into the middle of the room, twirled three times, and then posed for a moment before twirling once more.

Alice suddenly gave a loud squeal.

"Look!" she whispered. "That's my big sister!" And a dark-haired princess (she looked a lot like Alice) did an extra twirl right in front of us, and winked a tiny wink as she swirled out through the door.

As the last Tiara Club Princess

swept herself away, I found I was holding my breath. They were so beautiful, they made me feel a little odd . . .

Maybe I should tell you something, but it's a secret. Please don't tell anyone.

Ever since I was tiny, I've always wanted to be a Perfect Princess and join the Tiara Club. I really do try to be kind and helpful, not because I want to be a goody-goody, but because it's what princesses do. Seeing the Tiara Club Princesses made me remember that I'd shouted at Perfecta. It made me feel like a total failure. *How would I ever get to join the Tiara Club if I behaved like that?* I made myself a promise to try much harder.

The Duchess was glowing. She was so pleased we liked her dresses. "And now it's your turn," she said. "Just remember that every speck of dirt will show on the white, so please be careful." And she handed each of us a piece of paper, a pencil, a package of needles and thread, and a huge pair of scissors.

I started to panic when Duchess Delia gave me those scissors. I could just imagine enormous piles of ruined velvet, and me with nothing to wear . . . but I'd forgotten that Fairy G. had magic powers.

It was fantastic! We each drew our ideal dress (Duchess Delia came over and helped us), and then

Fairy G. tapped the material we'd chosen with her wand, and immediately the scissors zoomed off all on their own and cut out the shapes perfectly! And then the needles sewed up our dresses with such tiny stitches you could hardly

see them. And the best part was that if something looked wrong, you just erased your picture, and drew your dress a different way, and—*tingle zingle!*—the scissors and the needles fixed it!

Chapter Four

$\mathcal{B}$y the time the lunch bell rang, we were all positively buzzing with excitement. The Sewing Room tables were piled high with beautiful dresses and hoops and petticoats and sashes . . . but one thing was really weird.

Perfecta was behaving as if she was the most amazingly Perfect Princess ever! When I dropped my needle, she practically jumped to pick it up—and she threaded it for me. And she kept saying how fabulous my dress was.

Of course, Duchess Delia thought

Perfecta was wonderful.

"*Such* a kind, thoughtful, generous girl," she said. "I shall give you twenty tiara points right now!"

Perfecta curtsied very low . . . but as she got up again I'm *almost* sure I saw her wink at Floreen.

We finally managed to get away from Perfecta in the lunch line, and Charlotte immediately said, "What's going on?"

"She's up to something," Katie said darkly. "She was winking at Floreen."

"I suppose she might have decided to try and be good," Daisy said. "After all, Fairy G. *did* give her a huge warning at breakfast."

"But that was before she had lashed out at me and Sophia," Alice pointed out.

Emily rubbed her nose. "It's very

strange. Hey, what do you think the surprise is?"

"I think it's some kind of outdoor party," Alice said. "That white velvet's really thick!"

"But it's not cold outside," Daisy said. "The sun's shining!"

"I guess we'll have to wait and see." Emily sighed. "Maybe Fairy G. will tell us after lunch."

But Fairy G. didn't. She said she had important business to take care of, and she'd see us later.

We spent the afternoon decorating our dresses. Duchess Delia brought in baskets of rainbow-colored beads and feathers and ribbons (they looked fabulous on the white dresses!), and bunches of little silk roses in all kinds of pastel colors. And Perfecta went on being amazingly perfect. She let me take the one and only bunch of pink silk roses, and I know she wanted them really badly for herself, because she practically snatched them out of the basket. She even helped me pin the pink roses onto the front of my dress.

"There!" she said. "Don't they look beautiful?"

They did, and I thanked Perfecta as enthusiastically as I

could, but my brain was doing somersaults.

Could Daisy possibly be right? Was Princess Perfecta really and truly trying to be good?

"Look! It's snowing!"

Princess Freya was waving her

arms in excitement, and I forgot all about Perfecta as I dashed to the window to look.

Freya was right. Huge white snowflakes were tumbling from the sky, and the Academy looked like a magical, fairy palace.

"But it's the wrong time of year!" Princess Lisa said. "It *can't* snow now!"

Duchess Delia laughed. "It can do whatever Fairy G. tells it to do, dear! Have you seen the lake?"

We stared and stared. The lake

had frozen into a sparkling silver mirror.

"Oh!" Alice clapped her hands. "A skating party!"

"Exactly, my dear," Duchess Delia said. "A Sparkling Ice Extravaganza! Now, all of you finish your dresses and hang them on the rail. You're to go downstairs for an early dinner, and then come back to change and get ready. As you go outside, you will each be given a pair of ice skates and a muff. And then you should all enjoy yourselves!"

Chapter Five

I was the last to leave the Sewing Room. Everyone else tumbled out in a chattering rush, but I waited behind. I'd made a decision.

Duchess Delia asked me what was wrong.

"Please," I said, and I curtsied.

"I'd like to surprise Princess Perfecta. I was very mean to her this morning—so would it be all right if I let her have the pink silk roses for her dress? I know she'd like them."

"What a nice girl you are!" Duchess Delia cooed. "Just the perfect friend for dear Perfecta! Of course you may put the roses on her dress—here, let me help you." She whipped out a needle and thread and stitched the roses onto Perfecta's dress, just the way they'd been on mine.

"Perfect for Perfecta." She smiled at me. "And I know she

loved your dress, Sophia dear, so let's just give hers a couple of extra little tweaks, shall we?" Duchess Delia pinned and tucked and stitched. In two minutes, Perfecta's dress was frilled and gathered and looped exactly like mine.

"There!" said Duchess Delia. "The dear girl was so busy taking care of you and your friends that she never took time to think about herself. She'll have such a nice surprise!" Then Duchess Delia wafted away down the stairs, and I went down to the dining hall.

Of course all of the Rose Room Princesses wanted to know what I'd been doing.

"Honestly," Charlotte said when I told her. "You're just *too* nice, Sophia. Why should Perfecta have the roses *and* the prettiest dress? She's only been good for one day!"

"She's up to something," Katie added.

"She was mean at breakfast," Emily said. "Why are you being so nice to her?"

I looked down at my feet. "You'll think I'm stupid."

Alice shook her head. "No we won't."

"We're your friends!" Daisy said.

"Well," I said slowly. "I kept thinking about what I said at breakfast. About Perfect Princesses thinking about others before themselves, and being kind. Even if Perfecta *was* awful, that didn't mean I had to be awful back."

When dinner was over, we went back to the Sewing Room, which was full of giggling first years sitting at the tables. Fairy G. and Duchess Delia were already looking wonderfully grand as they stood in front of the rack of beautiful winter ballgowns.

"What's up with Perfecta?" Charlotte whispered in my ear. "Does she know about her dress?"

Perfecta did look very pink, and her eyes were gleaming.

"I don't think so," I said. At that very moment, Fairy G. held up the first dress.

"One truly beautiful dress decorated with pink silk roses! Tell me, who does this belong to?"

I raised my hand. "Fairy G.,

that belongs to Princess Perfecta!" I took an extra-deep breath. "And I'd like to say I'm sorry I was so awful to her this morning, and I hope she'll forgive me!"

There was an amazed silence, and then Perfecta leaped to her feet.

"No—it's not! It's *not* my dress! It's Sophia's!"

Duchess Delia smiled a big smile. "Aha! But that's where you're wrong, Perfecta dear! Look! Sophia and I have put the pink roses on *your* dress as a surprise! *This* is Sophia's dress." She picked the next dress off the rack and lifted it up. We all gasped.

There was a huge black stain
right down the front. It looked
terrible!

Nobody said anything. We were much too shocked. Fairy G. looked grim as she picked up the next dress. It was covered in ink as well. And the next one. *And* the next . . . In fact, the one and only dress without a mark on it was Perfecta's.

"Princess Perfecta," Fairy G.

said, and she looked at Perfecta in a meaningful way, "can you explain why the only dress without any ink is yours?"

Perfecta's face turned green, and then she shrieked, "But it's *not* my dress! It *is* Sophia's! Isn't it, Floreen?"

Floreen nodded. "Yes. And it

proves she's guilty! She ruined all the other dresses, but she wouldn't ruin her own—"

Fairy G. stared at Floreen. Then she asked in a very scary voice, "And *why* should Princess Sophia want to ruin everyone else's dresses, Princess Floreen?"

"Because she's a show-off," Floreen said indignantly. "She thinks she's the best at everything. Perfecta said it would serve her right if everyone hated *her* for a change, instead of . . ." Her voice died away, and she turned bright red.

You can just imagine the noise.

Everybody was talking at once. Fairy G. had to swell up to her largest size and bellow before we were quiet.

"*Right!*" she boomed. "Princess Perfecta and Princess Floreen! Go

straight to Queen Gloriana's study!" And she shooed the two miserable princesses out, but then she stopped, and beamed her enormous smile.

"Ooops!" she said. "I nearly forgot!" She waved her wand, and at once every single ink stain vanished!

"There!" she said. "Better than new!"

Duchess Delia shook her head. "I'm shocked," she said, "really shocked. But now, let's see how you look in your gowns!"

Chapter Six

*T*he Sparkling Ice Extravaganza was so lovely! Tiny icicle lights twinkled on every tree, and the silver frozen lake reflected the millions of stars shining in the dark sky. Our ice skates were snow-white, like our dresses, and our muffs were made of the softest white fur (not real, of course!), sprinkled with shimmering pearls. A wonderful orchestra was already playing on a silver bandstand, and a full moon shone above. The music was glorious! We spun and

we twirled, and when it came to the polka, we practically *flew* over the ice. And then our principal, Queen Gloriana, came gliding out like a beautiful swan. She sailed into the middle of us, and the music stopped as she held up her hand.

"I don't want to keep you from your fun," she told us, "but I have a special award to make. Earlier today, Princess Sophia was carried away by her desire to protect a friend from an unkind attack which, I regret to say, came from two other princesses here at the Academy. Like any true princess, Sophia realized her mistake, and did her best to set things right with a gift and an apology. Sadly, the two princesses had already decided to take an unpleasant revenge on Sophia for her outspokenness. That matter is now being dealt with, but I would very much like

to recognize, here at the Sparkling Ice Extravaganza, Princess Sophia's most excellent example of how to be a Perfect Princess, and I hereby award her fifty tiara points! And now, music please!"

Queen Gloriana gave me a dazzling smile, and, as I sank into my deepest curtsey, she sailed away across the ice. And do you know what? I felt exactly as if I was sparkling inside and out, and as

Alice and Charlotte and Emily and Daisy and Katie and I held hands to swing around and around, I really did believe that one day I'd be a Perfect Princess and win my place in the Tiara Club—and you'll be there too. I just *know* you will!

What happens next?

FIND OUT IN

Princess Emily
∞ AND THE ∞
Substitute Fairy

Hi there! I'm Princess Emily—one of the Rose Room Princesses from the Princess Academy. Do you know Alice, and Katie, and Daisy, and Charlotte, and Sophia? They're my best friends—just like you! And have you met Princess Perfecta yet? She's awful. Alice says it's because some people are just born that way—they can't help being nasty.

All the same, I wish Perfecta wasn't in our class. But at least I have my best friends—and you!

you are cordially invited to vis
www.tiaraclubbooks.com!

Visit your special princess friends
at their dazzling website!

Find the secret word hidden in each of the first six Tiara Cl
books. Then go to the Tiara Club website, enter the sec
word, and get an exclusive poster. Print out the poster
each book and save it. When you have all six, put the
together to make one amazing poster of the entire Ro
Princess Academy. Use the stickers in the books to decor
and make your very own perfect princess academy poster.

More fun at www.tiaraclubbooks.com

- Download your own Tiara Club membership card!

- Win future Tiara Club books.

- Get activities and coloring sheets with every new book

- Stay up-to-date with the princesses in this great series!

Visit www.tiaraclubbooks.com and be a part of the Tiara Cl